A House for Little Red

DEAR CAREGIVER,

The *Beginning-to-Read* series is a carefully written collection of classic readers you may remember from your own childhood. Each book features text comprised of common sight words to provide your child ample practice reading the words that appear most frequently in written text. The many additional details in the pictures enhance the story and offer the opportunity for you to help your child expand oral language and develop comprehension.

Begin by reading the story to your child, followed by letting him or her read familiar words and soon your child will be able to read the story independently. At each step of the way, be sure to praise your reader's efforts to build his or her confidence as an independent reader. Discuss the pictures and encourage your child to make connections between the story and his or her own life. At the end of the story, you will find reading activities and a word list that will help your child practice and strengthen beginning reading skills.

Above all, the most important part of the reading experience is to have fun and enjoy it!

Shannon Cannon

Shannon Cannon,
Literacy Consultant

Norwood House Press • P.O. Box 316598 • Chicago, Illinois 60631
For more information about Norwood House Press please visit our website at *www.norwoodhousepress.com* or call 866-565-2900.

LIBRARY OF CONGRESS CATALOGING-IN-PUBLICATION DATA

Hillert, Margaret.
 A house for Little Red / by Margaret Hillert ; illustrated by Kelly Oechsli.—
Rev. and expanded library ed.
   p. cm. — (Beginning to read series. Easy stories)
 Summary: A boy plays with his dog and provides a house for him. Includes reading activities.
  ISBN-13: 978-1-59953-029-1 (library edition : alk. paper)
  ISBN-10: 1-59953-029-5 (library edition : alk. paper)
 [1. Dogs—Fiction. 2. Readers.] I. Oechsli, Kelly, ill. II. Title. III. Series.
 PZ7.H558Ho 2006
 [E]—dc22   2005033394

A Beginning-to-Read Book

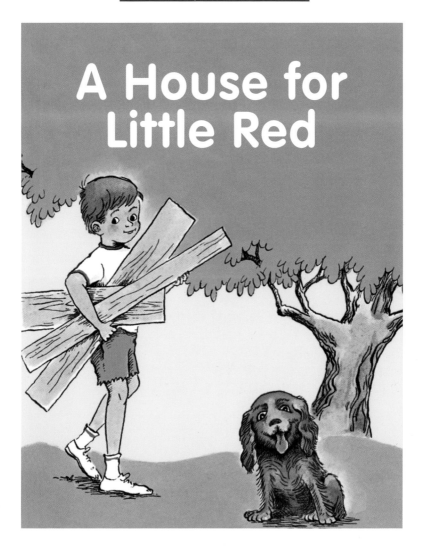

A House for Little Red

by Margaret Hillert

Illustrated by Kelly Oechsli

NORWOOD HOUSE PRESS

Here, Red.
Here, Red.
Come here, Little Red.

Come here to me, Little Red.
Run, run, run.
Here is a cookie for you.

I want to play.
We can run and jump.

One, two, three.
Here we go.

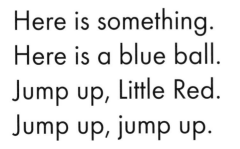

Here is something.
Here is a blue ball.
Jump up, Little Red.
Jump up, jump up.

Go, Red go.
Go and find the ball.

Oh look, Red.
Look here.
Here is something for a house.
I can make a house for you.

Go in, Red.
Go into the house.

Oh, oh.
It is not a house.
You look funny.

Here is a yellow house.
Go in here.
Go in, go in.

Oh my, oh my.
The house is down.
It is not for you.

Come, Little Red.
Come and look.
We can find a house.

Here is a little house.
I see something in it.
One, two, three little ones.
It is not for you, Red.

Look up, look up.
I see a house up here.
Oh, my.
It is not for you.

Look here, Red.
Look down here.
Here is a little house.
See the mother.
You can not go in here.

Come, Red.
Come away.
It is not for you.

Oh, here is Father.
Father is big.
Father can help.

Father, Father.
Can you make a house?
Can you make a house for Little Red?

I can. I can.
Come and see.
I can work.
You can help me.

Down, Red, down.
You can not work.
You can not help.
Go away.

Oh, Father.
The house is big.
Where is Red?
Come, Red.
Go into the house.

LITTLE RED

Red is in the house.
A big house.
A blue house.
A house for Little Red.

The following activities support the findings of the National Reading Panel that determined the most effective components for reading instruction are: Phonemic Awareness, Phonics, Vocabulary, Fluency, and Text Comprehension.

Phonemic Awareness: The /ou/ diphthong

Oddity Task: Say the /ou/ -as in h**ou**se- sound for your child. Ask your child to say the word that doesn't have the /ou/ sound in the following word groups:

house, out, hand	round, run, hour	shout, snout, short
moose, mouse, mouth	sour, sound, sort	paint, pout, proud

Phonics: The letters o, u

1. Demonstrate how to form the letters **o** and **u** for your child.

2. Have your child practice writing **o** and **u** at least three times each.

3. Ask your child to point to the words in the book that have the letters **ou** in them.

4. Write down the following words and spaces and ask your child to write ou in the spaces to complete each word:

h__ __ se	m__ __ se	__ __ t	__ __ r
fl__ __ r	c__ __ ch	s__ __ th	r__ __ nd
c__ __ nt	b__ __ nce	cl__ __ d	s__ __ nd

5. Ask your child to read each completed word, provide help sounding them out as needed.

Vocabulary: Animal Homes

1. Write the following words on separate pieces of sticky note paper:

   bird   duck   bear   horse   bat   chicken   bee

   hive   coop   pond   den   nest   cave   barn

2. Read each word for your child.

3. Mix up the words and ask your child to match the animal names with the correct home.

Fluency: Choral Reading

1. Reread the story with your child at least two more times while your child tracks the print by running a finger under the words as they are read. Ask your child to read the words he or she knows with you.

2. Reread the story aloud together. Be careful to read at a rate that your child can keep up with.

3. Repeat choral reading and allow your child to be the lead reader and ask him or her to change from a whisper to a loud voice while you follow along and change your voice.

Text Comprehension: Discussion Time

1. Ask your child to retell the sequence of events in the story.

2. To check comprehension, ask your child the following questions:

   • What kind of houses does the boy make for Little Red?

   • What animal houses does the little boy find?

   • Why do you think the little boy wants to get a house for Little Red?

   • Do you have a pet? If so, what do you do to take care of your pet? If not, what kind of pet would you like and what would you do to take care of it?

WORD LIST

A *House for Little Red* uses the 49 words listed below.

This list can be used to practice reading the words that appear in the text. You may wish to write the words on index cards and use them to help your child build automatic word recognition. Regular practice with these words will enhance your child's fluency in reading connected text.

a	go	make	the
and		me	three
away	help	mother	to
	here	my	two
ball	house		
big		not	up
blue	I		
	in	oh	want
can	into	one (s)	we
come	is		where
cookie	it	play	work
down	jump	red	yellow
		run	you
father	little		
find	look		
for		see	
funny		something	

ABOUT THE AUTHOR Margaret Hillert has written over 80 books for children who are just learning to read. Her books have been translated into many different languages and over a million children throughout the world have read her books. She first started writing poetry as a child and has continued to write for children and adults throughout her life. A first grade teacher for 34 years, Margaret is now retired from teaching and lives in Michigan where she likes to write, take walks in the morning, and care for her three cats.

Photograph by Glenna Washburn

ABOUT THE ADVISER Shannon Cannon contributed the activities pages that appear in this book. Shannon serves as a literacy consultant and provides staff development to help improve reading instruction. She is a frequent presenter at educational conferences and workshops. Prior to this she worked as an elementary school teacher and as president of a curriculum publishing company.